The
Tent

also by gary paulsen

gary paulsen

The

Tent:

a parable in one sitting

harcourt brace & company
San Diego   New York   London

Requests for permission to make copies of any part of the work should be
mailed to: Permissions Department, Harcourt Brace & Company,
6277 Sea Harbor Drive, Orlando, Florida 32887-6777.

Library of Congress Cataloging-in-Publication Data
Paulsen, Gary.
The tent: a parable in one sitting/by Gary Paulsen.—1st ed.
p.   cm.
Summary: Although dismayed and embarrassed when his father takes
him on the road to get rich preaching the word of God, fourteen-year-
old Steven finds himself caught up in the money and the things it
can buy.
ISBN 0-15-292879-0
[1. Evangelists—Fiction.]   I. Title.
PZ7.P2843Te   1995
[Fic]—dc20   94-36103

The text was set in Perpetua.
Designed by Lisa Peters

B C D E
Printed in the United States of America

The
Tent

In the eighth century B.C.E. in what is now Israel/Palestine, the birthplace and stipulations of a religious leader were prophesied. He was to be born in the village called Bethlehem, of a virgin.

In the small town of Nazareth, a pregnant teenage girl was engaged to a carpenter. During this time the Romans called for a census, and because the carpenter was from the house of David, he took his fiancée to the town of Bethlehem to register. All of the inns were full due to the increased number of people in town, but he was able to obtain lodging in a stable, and it was there the baby was born.

From Bethlehem the family moved to Egypt for a short time and then back to the district of Galilee to Nazareth. This was where the baby grew up as the eldest son of the carpenter.

He began teaching at the age of thirty, choosing his first followers from the area of Galilee. He taught among the poor and the sick, explaining to people how to love God in truth and not just for appearance, and to love their neighbors as much as themselves.

His most radical teaching was that man was sinful and in need of salvation (saving) and that just doing good things was not enough to justify man before a holy God.

The people had expected a different sort of messiah, one who would save them from Roman oppression, and this man didn't fit that description. He spent his time telling stories, not raising an army. Still the leaders were concerned about the large crowds that he attracted and the things he had to say about the religious leaders of the day.

Within three short years, by the age of thirty-three, the young man had enraged the religious community to the point that the religious leaders had him arrested and brought before the high priest on charges of blasphemy—a crime punishable by death. The chief priests did not have the power to execute the death penalty so they handed him over to the Roman governor, saying the man and his followers were political subversives. The sentence handed down was death, to be carried out by the then normal official mode of execution, death by crucifixion.

Even though he had predicted his own death, his followers were downhearted and most were in hiding, fearing for their own lives. Then news came

For where your treasure is,
there will your heart
be also.

"I figure it this way," his father said one evening. "I'm thirty-four years old and we don't have a pot to pee in or a window to throw it out of to call our own. How do you see it?"

Steven shrugged. "I don't think it's that bad."

"We live in a ten-year-old rented trailer in a trailer park," his father, who was named Corey, cut in. "We're driving a nineteen sixty-seven Chevy half-ton with salt rot so bad you can read through it. We don't have any money—and I mean *any*—your mother has gone off with a . . . well . . . a friend, and you just got a pair of Salvation Army tennis shoes for your fourteenth birthday, and you don't think it's *bad?*"

"You've got a job."

"At minimum wage. I can't even pay the rent on this trailer without working two full-time base-wage jobs."

Steven stopped. He'd heard some of this before but never as far down as his father sounded now. Not even when his mother had gone. They were close, he and his father—somehow being poor had brought them closer.

His father had not always been this poor. They had lived in Kansas City, and for as long as Steven could remember—until he was twelve—his father had worked at a factory that made doors. Then the factory had closed down and gone to another country—Steven thought Mexico—and even his father, who had been a foreman of a whole shift, was terminated. That had been two years earlier when Steven was twelve. And for a time his father had been positive. He'd taken schooling, learned a new job—in, of all things, shoe repair—and started a new life. They had moved to Texas and settled in to find work. But there were no good jobs. Nobody was hiring people to repair shoes, and there was no decent work anywhere. None.

And it had stayed bad until this evening, when he listened to his father go further down than he'd ever heard.

"I can work," Steven said. "I'll get a job."

His father nodded. "I figured you'd say that. So I kind of thought you wouldn't mind helping me."

Steven had been half watching the television with the sound on mute. But there was a new note in his father's voice—something that sounded soft, almost not there. Like he had a secret.

"What are you talking about?" Steven asked.

"I'm sick of being poor," his father said. "Aren't you?"

A new feeling—cold, chill. Steven turned the set off. An old one, so old it was only black-and-white, seven inches diagonally, so old it made a bright spot in the middle when it went off. The set was suddenly very important. He remembered when they got it. Twelve dollars. At a pawn shop.

"Are you talking about something illegal?" *There, he thought—I asked it.* It had to be asked. "Like stealing or something . . . ?"

And his father had smiled. "No. Not illegal at all. We're going to help people."

"Help them?"

A nod, very slowly. "Yes. We're going to help them find God."

"God?" Steven stared at his father. In fourteen years Steven had never heard his father mention God—not counting the time he'd slammed his thumb with a framing hammer. They had never been to church, never studied the Bible, never spoken of anything even remotely religious. Steven didn't know what else to say. Just that, the question—*God?*

"Sure. Look, there's people out there by the thousands who are having trouble finding God. I'm just saying we help them."

"But how . . . I mean why . . . no, what? Yes, that's it—what are you going to do?"

"I," his father said, raising his voice, "am going to preach."

"Preach?"

"The Word of God." His father's voice rose higher, louder, bounced off the walls of the trailer. "I aim to preach the Word of God—the *Word* of God, the Word of *God!*" He stopped suddenly and then smiled, lowered his voice to a conversational tone. "And I want you to help me."

"Me?" Steven's head was reeling. He was convinced his father was insane. "You want me to help preach?"

His father laughed. "Not exactly. Look now—I mean listen. When I got out of the army I had a friend named Farnham. He was sick of being poor, and he told me he was going to find an old tent and go around preaching in small towns. He wanted me to go with him, and I came very close—even listened to him talk about how he would do his spiel, bark the Word, as they used to say in the old carny days. I was even packed. But I met your mother and got married and we had you, and I never saw Farnham again."

"Well, then how—"

"But I *heard* from him. About a year later he sent me a picture of himself. He was wearing a powder blue linen suit, standing next to a powder blue new Cadillac. On the back he wrote just one sentence, 'I'm rich!' and that was all I ever heard from him. . . ."

A million questions roared through Steven's head, but before he could form any of them into words, his father was off again.

"I've got it all worked out," he said, leaning forward on the table. "That roofer O'Malley owes me three hundred for helping him four weekends. He doesn't have the money but he *does* have an old army tent he got from a guy for work. It's not huge—thirty by forty—but that's big enough for a start. And it comes with a string of lights to hang on the inside. I'll make a plywood pulpit and a little stand to make me higher—you've got to be higher than your flock to force them to look up—and we're in business."

"We are?"

"Yup. I'll get a white collar, and I've got that old dark sports jacket and those pants I never wear. Slick back my hair and grab the Bible—where *is* the Bible, by the way?"

"We don't have one."

"Oh. Well, no matter. We can get one in the first motel we stay at. Every room has one of those Gideon Bibles. We'll take one of those."

And that was, exactly, how it all started, with a Bible stolen from a cheap motel room.

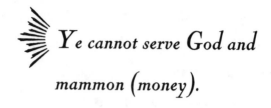 *Ye cannot serve God and mammon (money).*

IT DID NOT initially go well.

"Man, there's a lot of stuff in here."

They were in the kitchen area of the small trailer—a table that was bolted to the wall and folded down when they wanted more room. Steven was sitting, still in a kind of stunned wonder, staring at the table. There was a road map of Texas spread out, a small pad of paper and a pen, and his father had the Bible, which he had opened on top of the map. He was looking at the Bible, frowning.

"It's packed with things—how is a man supposed to find something to preach about?"

Steven coughed. "You can't be serious about all this."

"About what?"

"Doing this preaching thing. I thought you were kidding."

"I got the Bible, didn't I?"

Steven nodded. "Yes . . ."

"And I didn't even have to pay for the room. I told them I wanted to check the room out for friends who were coming, and the Bible was lying right there, and we saved nearly thirty dollars because we didn't need to rent the room."

"Well . . ."

"And we got the tent, didn't we?"

Steven nodded again. They *had* gotten the tent, although it was somewhat the worse for wear. It had been an army tent used for assembling missiles in some forgotten day and had holes in the top and two round openings, one at either end, for the missile to stick out. "It will leak," Steven pointed out. "Top, sides, and ends. You could throw a basketball through the walls."

"That doesn't matter," his father said. "We have the tent. We have the Bible. We're serious. We're going to do this thing and get rich."

The truth was, at that stage, Steven was horrified. He was not good around people, almost shy, knew nothing of religion, and still thought there was a good chance his father had gone completely mad. He'd heard about it on the news. Stress did it. They talked about it all the time. He needed to learn stress management. *Maybe,* Steven thought, *I can get him involved in one of those classes. . . .*

"I think we're going to have to pick one subject and stick to it." His father nodded to himself. "At least until we get a handle on this thing. What's a good subject?"

"Pardon?"

"To preach—give me a subject. We need something to talk about."

Steven stared at him. "How about lying?"

"Lying . . ."

"Or stealing. You know, like where you steal a Bible and lie about being a preacher."

"Oh. You feel that way about it?"

Steven looked out the small window of the trailer. In the trailer next to theirs the couple—he never knew their names—who drank cheap beer and fought all the time were drinking cheap beer and fighting. The woman finished a bottle of beer and threw the empty bottle at her husband, who swore and emptied his own and threw it at her. Luckily they were both so drunk they missed. "I don't know how to feel. This is all too new for me to feel anything."

"Look, I've been watching these guys on television. Do you think they're all sincere?"

"I've never watched them. Well, once, when the guy cried all the time. I don't know what they think."

"They do it for the money. But that doesn't mean it's all bad. If we do it for the money but we say good things, what's wrong with that? We get money, they get something. We all come out ahead."

"But we don't know anything, we don't believe all that stuff, and we've never even been to church." The couple next door opened new beers. They kissed. They were hugging now. "It's all a lie."

"But a good lie. We're doing it for good reasons, right?"

Steven didn't say anything, shrugged.

"Right. We get some money, they get some preaching. Perfect. The thing is, I can't do it all alone. There's too much going on. I need you to help me—so will you?"

Another long pause. "Well, I guess so. . . ."

"So give me a subject. A good one, one I can really get my teeth into and preach the hell out of."

Steven smiled. "So what's wrong with lying and stealing? Like I said?"

His father thought for half a minute, then shook his head. "Not enough. It needs more meat to it.

That's a good start, but it needs to be filled out. We need something about specific sins—sex, killing. Like that."

Steven looked out the window again and spoke absently, without thinking—he was still reeling from what his father was planning to do. "Talk about somebody who lies about sex."

His father frowned, then nodded. "Yes. I like that. I'll work on that angle." He turned back to the Bible. "Now, how do you find all that in here? Is there some kind of index, you know, in back where they have subjects? L for *lying,* S for *sex . . .*"

Steven stood and went to the sink for a drink of water while his father flipped through the Bible. All the while Steven was trying to think of a way out of going, but nothing came and he knew he was locked into helping. He sighed. Might as well act interested. "Where are we going?"

His father looked up. "What?"

"The first town—where are we going to start all this?"

"I don't know. I thought I'd kind of wing it. Not too far, though—we don't have much money for gas and the truck is definitely terminal." He drew a finger in a circle on the map around the trailer park. "Somewhere in here—inside a hundred-mile circle."

Steven moved back to the table, studied the map, pointed. "There—let's go there."

"Where? Oh . . . out there. Castle, Texas. Why there?"

"Just the name—Castle—seems like a good place to start."

"All right—that's it. We'll go day after tomorrow."

And, Steven thought, looking at the location of the town, *it might be far enough that I will never see anybody who lives there again.*

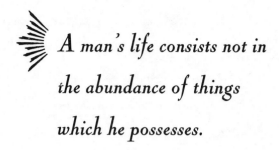 *A man's life consists not in
the abundance of things
which he possesses.*

IT WASN'T—quite—a disaster.

Castle was a small town that could be described mostly by the words *flat* and *hot*. They drove through miles of feedlots full of cattle to get there—the stink of manure so thick Steven had trouble breathing—and when they came to Castle they had almost driven through it before they realized it was the town.

"I don't know," his father said. "There aren't many people here."

Perfect, Steven thought. "They live around the town—on ranches and things. It will do fine."

On the west side of town there was a small park

with an open area next to it, and they pulled the old truck in and unloaded the tent.

It weighed close to two hundred pounds and Steven doubted that they would be able to get it raised and set—and was looking forward to failing and returning home—but two men in cowboy hats showed up.

"What are you doing?" One of them, sipping a Dr Pepper, scratched and spit. "A flea market?"

Steven's father turned from wrestling the tent out of the back of the truck. "We are here," he said, lowering his voice and somehow raising it at the same time, "to preach the Word of God."

Both men nodded, and the second one smiled. "Been close to two weeks since we've had a tent preacher here. What faith are you?"

"Faith?"

"Yeah. Baptist or Evangelical Missionary or rollers or what?"

"We are of God," Steven's father said. "We do

not believe in different faiths—we are all one children."

Steven couldn't help staring. It didn't even
sound like his father.

"Now," his father continued, "if you would
kindly help us set up this . . . traveling chapel . . .
we'd appreciate it."

With all four working, the tent went up in forty
minutes and they stood back to view it.

"Kind of . . . ventilated . . . ain't it?" one of the
cowboys said.

To Steven it looked a lot like a large piece of
ratty canvas swiss cheese, but his father nodded.

"For air movement," he said. "Keeps it cool
when all the people pack in."

They had eight benches, four for each side,
made of boards and square boxes to hold them off
the ground, and Steven set the benches up while his
father arranged the plywood pulpit in the front. In a
moment of artistic fervor he had cut a cross—it

looked crooked to Steven—from thick wood and painted it red and put it on the front of the pulpit, and the red cross glared out at them.

"There," he said, when it was done. "Now we have to spread the word."

They finished in an hour, covering the town with the small posters they had made on a copier at the library for ten cents a copy. There seemed to be one on every pole, fence, and wall Steven could see.

"There." His father rubbed his hands together. "Now we wait."

The afternoon dragged slowly by. Steven, who thought he had never been so mortally embarrassed, had gone into a kind of shock. He sat on the shady side of the tent—the Texas sun was almost flash hot—and tried not to think, but it was impossible. All along he had operated on the premise that it would never happen; something or somebody would intervene and stop it before it actually came to pass.

But the tent was up, the posters were in place, and as slowly as the time passed, it *did* pass.

And for the first time in his life Steven prayed.

"Please, God, don't let anybody come to this tonight."

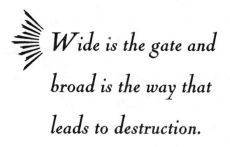

*Wide is the gate and
broad is the way that
leads to destruction.*

IT WAS A SCENE, Steven thought, that looked like it was shot on a cheap home video for a very bad movie.

The tent, even with the ends opened, was viciously, unbelievably hot. His father had put on the dark sports jacket and slacks—both originally purchased at Goodwill for two dollars—and had used a piece of white cardboard to make a minister's collar. But the coat was a thick one, made for winter, and Steven estimated the temperature in the tent to be at least 120 degrees. He could hardly breathe, and his father was completely soaked in perspiration, standing at the front of the tent in the gloomy light coming from the evening sun (there was no power outlet for the string of lights) with his hands clasped piously in front, waiting for worshipers to start coming.

They had put 7:00 P.M. as the time to start, and as the deadline came closer, Steven began to hope his prayer had been answered. Even the two cowboys who had been there this afternoon failed to come.

But at precisely seven there was a horrendous clatter and two ancient pickups arrived filled with people—or so it seemed. There were six adults. Two men somewhere close to forty, both wearing bib overalls and clean denim work shirts, both sunburned beet red in the face with a line on their foreheads where their caps stopped the sun. They could have been brothers. With them were four women, two of them wives and two who appeared to be grandmothers. The women were also sunburned, wearing clean but tired print dresses, and the backs of both trucks were filled with what seemed to be a herd of children. They were all dressed in tattered but clean clothes, all seemed to be scrubbed with rough brushes, and they never stopped moving. There were either eight of them or ten of them or—Steven closed one eye—maybe twelve.

They all filed into the tent and sat on the rough plank benches.

"Welcome," Steven's father said softly, "to the house of God."

"What did he say?" one of the grandmothers asked.

The man on her right leaned in close to her ear and bellowed, "HE SAID WELCOME TO THE HOUSE OF THE LORD!"

"Oh. Good."

The men turned to Steven's father. "You want to get loud on the good parts—ever since Granny was next to the water heater when it blew. Especially when the crowd comes."

"I will."

But as the moments passed and turned into a quarter of an hour—crawling moments while the small group waited on the benches—it became painfully apparent that there would not be a "crowd." Nobody else came. Worse, as time seemed to stop, the pack of kids became restless and started wrestling and tumbling—they looked like a rolling ball of arms and legs to Steven—until the same man turned and thumped three or four of them.

"You don't start preaching soon," he said, turning to the front, "and I'm going to have to get the rope and tie them to the truck."

Corey nodded but still hesitated, and Steven realized it was because he was nervous. Corey took a breath, held it, let it out, and spread his arms woodenly to the side.

"Friends . . . ," he croaked, his voice breaking. "We are gathered here in His name—"

"Louder!" The old woman bellowed.

"FRIENDS!" Steven's father began again. "WE ARE GATHERED HERE . . ."

And so it went. He had written what he called a

sermon, which he had on the plywood lectern, and had rehearsed in the trailer and while driving the truck so many times Steven almost knew it by heart. Corey followed the sermon, hollering each word at the top of his lungs, each word hitting Steven so loudly he winced.

". . . AND WE SHOULD NOT ASK FOR WHOM THE BELL TOLLS, IT TOLLS FOR THEE!" Corey finished, his voice now a rasp. He had been proud of the last line, which he had "borrowed" from a Hemingway novel, and he waited as though expecting applause.

None came and there was an embarrassed minute while everybody sat silent, seemingly waiting for something. Another minute and then Corey clapped his hands together.

"I almost forgot—the offering." He motioned to Steven to pass the basket.

Now Steven hesitated. The "basket" was a huge wicker affair that they had bought for a quarter at Goodwill. It was the kind of basket used for displaying fruit in grocery stores. *It could hold melons,* Steven thought, as he passed it to the people on the bench. He was so embarrassed, he failed to watch for money but turned away and went back to the side of the tent.

Because the basket was so large, they had to handle it with both hands, and the man who held it last set it on the bench in front of him, and then they all settled back again, waiting.

Steven knew it was finished and he saw his father shoot him a perplexed look. Then he looked back to the small group, back at Steven.

"We like to end with a good song," the man directly in front of Corey said. "Sort of like *dee-zert.*"

"Song?"

"A hymn," the man said, nodding. "Sort of to fortify us to go back out amongst the sinners."

"Oh." Corey looked at Steven again.

Steven shrugged, shook his head. He didn't know any hymns.

Then Corey smiled and nodded at the man. "Why don't you lead us in a hymn?"

"ROCK OF AGES!" the old woman screamed suddenly, so loud Steven and Corey jumped.

"All right," Corey started. "That sounds good."

"CLEFT FOR ME!" she wailed.

"I said it's all right . . ."

"LET ME HIDE MYSELF IN THEE!"

And Steven realized then that she was singing the hymn. He didn't know the words, and neither did Corey, but it didn't matter. She took a deep breath, gathered her family around her with a stern look, and they all finished the hymn, not singing so much as screaming, almost but not quite in tune. And when it was done, they all stood at once and filed out.

"Well . . ." Steven sat on the bench in front of the pulpit. "*Now* will you believe we can't do it?"

His father collapsed and sat on the edge of the plywood platform that held the pulpit. He looked absolutely whipped—the dark coat drenched with

sweat, his shoulders bowed and almost caved in—
and he smiled weakly.

"It's just that you don't really know how to do
this," Steven added. "I never thought you would
get this far. I thought you would give it up by
now. . . ." He trailed off because his father had
noticed the huge collection basket on the bench. He
leaned forward and pulled the basket to his lap,
looked inside, and his face broke into a smile.

"It's nothing to be ashamed of," Steven started
again. "You just weren't meant to be a preacher."

"Look at this." Corey reached into the basket
and held up a handful of paper money. Mostly ones,
but Steven could see some fives and the corner of a
ten-dollar bill peeking out.

His father dropped the basket and rifled through
the money.

"Look at it!" He fanned the bills. "Ten, fifteen,
eighteen, another ten—there's twenty-eight dollars
here!"

"There is?" Steven stood, came forward. "Twenty-eight? They didn't look like they had two quarters to rub together."

"You know how many burgers I have to fry in part-time jobs to clear twenty-eight dollars?"

"Well . . ."

"Or how many feet of cruddy floors I've got to mop?"

"No. But still, you didn't do very well at it, you know."

"Well? Boy, we did *great* at it. Praise God."

"Praise God?"

"From whom all blessings flow. Say, I like that. I heard it somewhere, but I think I'll use it in my next sermon. Yeah. Not right up front of course. Just bring it in toward the end, right before we take the collection—no, that's *offering*. I saw one of those television ministers and he always called it an offering."

"You're going to do this again?" Steven asked.

"Boy—we're just starting. We're going to go all the way to the top."

"Oh," Steven said. "Oh, good."

And if someone had told him then that he would come to enjoy it, would come to love it, Steven would have laughed in his face.

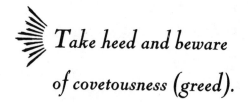

Take heed and beware of covetousness (greed).

THEY WENT across Texas, angling north, moving from small town to small town, but at first it did not seem to Steven to be getting any easier. Indeed, it seemed to be worse all the time.

The weather grew hotter, the humidity more steamy with each evening, and the air somehow more dusty. On the second stop—only thirty miles from the first town—they seemed to have gone to a different country. Steven thought it had been flat before but now the country became truly *flat*, impossibly so, and with the new flatness, the heat seemed to double in intensity.

They arrived early in the morning, having slept in the back of the truck, and set the tent up while it was still cool.

"I'll finish around here," Corey said, rubbing his hands together, "and you put up the posters."

Steven set off with the photocopies and tape. He had done four walls and three poles when a woman stopped him. She was perhaps fifty, although she looked ancient to Steven, and she wore a straight up-and-down dress like a suit of armor.

"What faith are you?" she demanded in a voice that was so brittle it seemed to crack.

"Pardon?"

"Of which faith be you?"

"Well, Christian, I guess, if it's all right that is."

"I *know* that. But are you of the rock in the mount or the fish?"

"I don't know. You'd have to ask my dad."

"Of the fish?"

"I don't know what you're talking about." *And neither,* he thought, *will Dad.* Then a stroke of what he thought to be genius hit him. "Why don't you come to the sermon tonight and find out?"

"Oh, we will, boy," she said, walking away. "We will."

We, Steven thought, watching her walk. *Who is* we?

By the time he finished putting up posters and returned to the tent, his father had set up the pulpit and benches and hidden the truck in back of some trees at the edge of the park they were using for the meeting.

Corey sat on a large rock on the shady side of the tent, writing in a notebook. Steven handed him a Coke he'd brought back from a small market and squatted next to him in the shade. "What are you doing?"

Corey took a long pull at the Coke, swallowed, and sighed. "We learned from the first one, right?"

Steven shrugged. "I'm not sure what, but yes, I guess we learned."

"We learned we have to have a sermon written down—that's one thing we learned."

"We also have to sing a hymn," Steven added. "And we have to sing it loud."

"I don't know a hymn, but while you were sticking up the posters I got a little tape recorder and a tape of a woman singing 'Amazing Grace.' You just play it at the right places," Corey said. "We'll memorize the words later so we can sing along." He paused, then sighed. "You know, if anybody comes . . ."

Steven suddenly remembered the woman who had stopped him but decided not to tell his father. There had been something about her voice, a hardness, and he wasn't sure he wanted Corey to worry.

"I'm half-wrecked," Corey said, putting the pencil down. "Why don't you watch things while I catch a quick nap in the truck."

He left and Steven sat quietly for a time, thinking of all the things he would rather be doing. The truth was there was nothing really to keep an eye on, and his attention quickly slid away. He flipped some rocks, waved at four people all crammed in the front seat of a pickup—pickups were everywhere, and very few cars—and was fast approaching a flat-line state in his thinking when his eyes closed and he fell asleep. When he opened them Corey was standing over him. It was dark, or nearly so—he must have been more tired than he thought—and Corey had found a power source on a pole at the edge of the park for the lights. "Come on, they're starting to arrive."

Steven stood and moved to the round tent opening.

They sat in a row on the bench, the new ones. Steven peered around the edge of the canvas at them. There were four—two men, two women, one the woman he had seen during the day—and they looked boiled, bleached, their eyes alert and somehow mean-looking.

Look out, Dad, he thought, *they're not taking prisoners.*

More cars trickled in, and finally there were twenty people who came in and sat on the benches. When Steven went to get his father from the truck, where he was putting his coat on, Corey smiled.

"How many?"

"Twenty."

"Twenty? Man, that's good. We stand to make some change tonight."

"Dad . . ." Steven thought about the four sitting on the front bench.

Corey had started for the tent and stopped. "What?"

And really there was nothing to tell—four people were sitting in the front row. What was that? "Nothing—good luck."

"Thanks." And he disappeared into the tent. Steven waited until Corey was at the pulpit, and turned the small tape player on. Scratchy notes from "Amazing Grace" fought to overcome the coughing and whispering sounds, and just as the music was to end, Steven turned the volume down to nothing in a slow fade. His father waited half a beat and turned to face the congregation.

"He lives," he said quietly.

"Amen."

"He lives for *all* sinners."

"Amen."

"Hallelujah!"

Steven turned away from the tent, or started to. He'd heard it all before when his father had rehearsed it. But halfway to the truck, a new voice stopped him.

"Be you of the *true* faith?" The voice was loud, challenging.

Corey stopped in the middle of a well-rehearsed sentence. "There are many faiths, brother," he said, his voice soft.

Here it comes, Steven thought, moving back toward the tent. *They'll get him now.* He peeked around the end just in time to see one of the four in front raise a finger and point directly at Corey.

"Yes—but are *you* of the *true* faith?" And now

the finger waved angrily. "Or do you blaspheme? Do you consort with low dwellers? Do you believe in God, the Son, and the Holy Ghost, or do you live with perverts and faggots and those consigned to burn for eternity?"

Steven could not believe the voice. It oozed, dripped hate, and he actually moved backward a step.

His father was taken aback as well and for a moment was quiet, could not seem to speak.

"I asked, do you believe?" The man's voice rose, became angrier, on the edge of vicious.

"I . . ."

"You do *not* believe!"

"We . . ."

"You do not *believe!*"

Again Corey hesitated, his mouth open, and Steven felt the fear in him, the discomfort, and started to move to him, to help him, to lead him from the tent and save him.

But a strange thing happened. Corey moved,

actually took a step back from the pulpit, seemed to retreat from the hate, and then changed, all in a second. His shoulders stiffened, his back straightened, and he raised his hands over his head.

"No!" Corey's voice was loud, filled the tent, and seemed to make the canvas flap at the sides. It was so sudden, it stopped the heckler. "I do *not* believe in hate, I do not *believe* in hate—God is a God of love. He loves all, all who come to Him. His love is in me, in you, in this holy tent." He took a breath, held it half a beat, and then, more softly, said, "I believe in love, the God of love who loves all things, all people, loves all. . . ."

And it worked. Steven stared at his father as he slid back into his rehearsed sermon. He was the same and yet somehow completely different. The tent was quiet, the people listening carefully to everything he said, and Steven watched, waiting for his cue to start the music for the offering hymn, and his father stayed in control the whole time.

Steven began the hymn and passed the basket

and was surprised to see all the people put bills in, even the one who had attacked Corey. As he played the final hymn, he glanced in the basket and saw several twenties and tens.

The people filed out, shaking hands with Corey at the tent opening, and Steven gathered the basket and counted the money. One hundred and fifty dollars and some change. He had moved out of the tent, and Corey came out. He was smiling strangely.

"Did you see that?"

"Dad—we made a lot of money. A hundred and fifty—"

"No—did you *see* that? My God, I owned them. They were in the palm of my hand. I think I could have taken them into a fire."

"But Dad—we made more—"

"Did you see it?" Corey wasn't listening. "Did you? Did you see it?"

And he walked away, smiling oddly, shaking his head slowly from side to side.

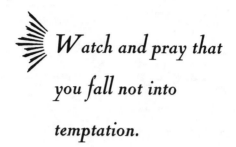 *Watch and pray that you fall not into temptation.*

IT SEEMED THEN that all things changed and nothing changed. What happened was so slow and subtle that Steven didn't often know it was happening until after it happened.

It came in stages, almost like scenes from a play or movie that Steven could only see after they happened and only understand after that, like when they went to Calypso.

Calypso, Texas, was small and dusty and flat, like much of Texas. They came into town well after dark and delayed setting up the tent until the next morning. Instead of sleeping in the truck, they took a room at a motel and had no sooner checked in then the phone rang.

"Hello?" Steven answered.

"I wish to speak to the minister. Is he there?"

"Yes?" Corey answered.

Then only short words.

"Yes. I agree. Yes. Please do. Fine. We'll expect you." And he hung up the phone.

"Some men are coming to talk to us," he said to Steven, "about how we can do better."

"Do better? We've only been doing this two weeks, and we're already making better than a hundred dollars a day. How can we do better?"

Corey smiled. "They told me about healing—using the Word to heal."

"Heal?"

Corey nodded. "They'll be here in a minute—they called from across the street."

And they were. Two men arrived within five minutes and knocked on the door softly. Corey let them in the room. One was short, balding, about forty and walked with a slight limp. The other was thin but not tall and had the start of a beard. Both men smiled at Steven, and he nodded to them and turned back to watching television, although he used the remote to cut the sound down.

"We like to help the gospelers," the bald man said. "We like to go assisting 'em to spread the Word."

Corey nodded. "So you said on the phone. Something about healing, you said."

The bald man nodded. "It's a true fact that you can do better if you throw in a healing—make twice as much."

"How do you mean?"

"Cripples, the blind, and the like. All you got to do is heal a couple of them, and those believers are going to *throw* money in the basket. It works every time."

Corey nodded. "I've seen healing on television. You just lay hands on them and they get healed, right?"

The bald man stood for a moment and didn't say anything.

"Isn't that the way it works? Their faith does the rest?"

"Well . . ." The bald man nodded. "You might say that. But they need a little help now and again, to get what you might call a clearer picture of their faith. They need some assistance. Me and Davis here like to think of ourselves as God's helpers. We sit in the congregation and when you call for the lame and halt and 'flicted I gets up and drags my leg—maybe you saw it when I came in here, the limp?—and come up with my hands all raised and crying, and you touch me and heal me and I walk away straight as a new pin."

Corey nodded. "And that gets the ball rolling?"

He shook his head. "One ain't enough, usually. There are them to waver in their faith, but two always does it. That's where Davis comes in. He has a good grating cough. Cough for 'em, Davis."

Davis, who had been silent all this time, nodded and coughed deep from his lungs. Even Steven had to admit it sounded serious, although he seemed none the worse for wear when he was done.

"That's a good cough," Corey said, nodding.

Jamey nodded. "He's got him a good lung cavity there. He was born with it. You can't just cough normal—anybody can do that. You've got to sound good. Davis here, when he's rolling good, sounds like he's about to heave a lung up. Then you lay hands on him and he breathes deep and that'll do her."

Steven was almost laughing out loud. It all sounded ridiculous and he expected Corey to throw them out any second, but when he looked at his father he was surprised to see interest.

"And you say this will help me increase the take—the flock?"

Jamey nodded. "We worked with a reverend name of Simmons down in the Corpus area, and he almost doubled his collections in a week. They come to see the miracles—they like them miracles more than anything."

"But won't they know you? I mean, you live around here. . . ."

Jamey shook his head. "Naw, we're from over in East Texas. We thought we'd come over here and see what there was to offer for a gimp and a lunger, and we seen you down below day before yesterday and liked the way you worked, so we thought we'd offer our assistance in the making of miracles."

"About that," Corey said. "Your assistance. How much . . . assistance . . . are we talking about here? How do you figure into the financial end of it?"

Jamey nodded, smiling. "I told Davis you'd get right to business. Well, I tell you, we used to just rely on the compassion of the trade, so to speak. But we found some ministers was more compassionate than others, and a lot of them weren't compassionate at all. So now we have a rate—we take fifteen percent of the collection."

"Fifteen? Isn't that a bit high?"

Jamey shrugged. "Depends on how you look at

it. If we double your collection then fifteen percent ain't so much, is it?"

"A good point."

"Let's do her this way," Jamey said. "You try us for three nights—one might not be enough—until the word gets out ahead that you found the power and you're doing some healing. If there ain't a good increase we part company and that's it. How does that sound?"

Corey nodded. "It sounds worth trying."

Corey and Jamey shook hands, Davis coughed, and the two men went to the door. Jamey stopped with his hand on the knob. "Are you open to some advice?"

Corey nodded. "What is it?"

"Your hair's too flat."

"My hair?"

"Yeah. You'll find them parishioners like a good head of hair on their reverends. You got to get it poofed up so it makes your head look big. It'd be good if it was silver or white, all combed up and back, but if you don't want to color it at least get it done to make it look bigger. You've got to have big hair to really get 'em into the faith."

"I'll see what I can do."

"Also you might want to buy some cheap shoes at a pawn shop and sand a hole in the bottom so they look worn. Then you want to sit down now and then and make sure they see the bottom of your shoes, so's they'll think you ain't doing all that well."

"Really? Do people really do that?"

Jamey nodded. "You've got to think to stay ahead, you've got to think all the time."

Jamey turned the doorknob, Davis went out in front of him, and they were gone. Steven watched them go and thought, *Now we've got a gimp and a lunger?*

Corey looked at the wall mirror over the small writing table next to the television. "You know, I think he's right. My hair *is* too flat. I believe I should have it done."

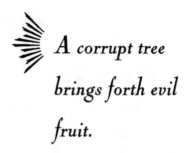

A corrupt tree brings forth evil fruit.

COREY WAS A natural at "healing," or as Jamey put it, "You can sure lay down them miracles."

That night there were thirty-four people—the best crowd they'd ever had—and none of them knew yet about the laying on of hands.

Jamey and Davis arrived slightly early, already "in character," as Jamey put it. Davis was coughing softly into a handkerchief with red spots on it.

"It's ketchup," Jamey said. "Holds the color better and lasts for hours." He was limping well, now and then dragging his right leg, and as a final touch had brought a pair of cheap wooden crutches. He spoke quietly for a few moments with Corey, who nodded, and then Jamey came to Steven, who was standing by the tent opening where the tape player was to play the opening hymn.

"Mind when I throw the crutches down," Jamey told Steven. "I'll throw them away from the congregation, but sometimes they'll get to being light-fingered, those who come to see the miracles. I've had crutches and even neck braces stole from me. So as soon as I flop them down you come on, you know, like an attendant and take them away."

"Like an attendant?"

"Exactly. We can't go to buying a new pair of crutches every night can we? It would eat the profits up."

"Profits . . ."

Jamey nodded, then smiled. "Ever wonder why *profits* and *prophets* sound so much alike? Kind of like a message, ain't it? Like we're supposed to be making money."

Steven moved back out the opening and out of sight, still smiling and half thinking it was all a joke.

But then people started to arrive and they all looked clean and hopeful, some of them kids, scrubbed and fresh and ready to hear about God, and a tinge of something, not a pain but coming toward it, a small shot of something cold and not very pretty came to him: they were doing this all to people who seemed to really believe.

But then it was time for the hymn to start and he became busy, and when the moment came for the laying on of hands and healing, everything was new and exciting and he forgot the feeling.

His father did the sermon and then they sang another hymn—Steven was getting good at keying in the music—but then, after the hymn, instead of passing the basket his father waved him away and stood at the pulpit again.

"I have heard there are those who need the heal-ing grace of God," he said.

"Amen," several in the congregation murmured. Steven was certain Davis and Jamey were first.

"Whoever you are, please come forward."

There was a moment's silence, almost an awkwardness that seemed to come into the tent and then a rustling as first Jamey, struggling on his crutches, and then Davis, the handkerchief to his mouth, came forward. They had been sitting at the end of the bench in the clear, but it was still difficult for Jamey to work the crutches around people's legs as he came forward, and he played it to the hilt, apologizing to them, stumbling, once falling nearly into somebody's lap.

Finally he stood before Corey, looking up at him, his eyes hopeful, and Steven could swear there was a tear coming down from each. "I want the power of God in me—I want Him to heal me."

"Do you believe?"

"I believe."

Corey stepped forward and put his hand on Jamey's forehead. "Do you *believe?*"

And he suddenly snapped Jamey's head back,

jerked it forward again, and Jamey stood silent for a moment, his eyes closed and then, almost in a whisper: "I feel it."

"Hallelujah," Corey said, also in a whisper.

Jamey half turned and said louder, "I feel it!"

"Hallelujah!" Corey made it louder, turned to the congregation, and raised his hands. "Hallelujah!"

"I feel the power of the Lord in me," Jamey said, louder still. "I feel it in my bones, in my old bones. I *feel* it."

"Amen," Corey said. Then, louder again, *"Amen!"*

And any hesitation in the people of the congregation, who had been almost silent, was gone when Jamey threw aside the crutches—being careful, as he'd said, to aim them away from the people where Steven could get them—and stood straight. "I'm healed! I'm *healed!"*

He turned and walked across the space in front of the pulpit without limping, and at the same time Davis started up with the most horrible hacking

Steven had ever heard, worse even than his demonstration in the motel room. He stumbled forward while he was coughing, the reddened handkerchief showing, and Corey repeated the gestures, shaking Davis's head and yelling, *"Heal!"*

Except by this time he had the crowd and they shouted, "Hallelujah!" and "Amen!" so loud Steven could almost see the canvas flapping, and when Davis stood and breathed deeply without coughing there was a continuous chorus of amens that fed on itself and grew until the tent was filled with sound.

Steven couldn't believe it. It was all so phony since he knew what was going on, but they wanted to believe in it so much, so very much, that they took it all at face value.

We are stealing from them, he thought. It struck him so hard that he actually took a step forward, was going to tell his father about the thought, but then something strange happened.

A woman stood up suddenly. She was tall and thin and seemed gaunt but not old. She was in the middle of the second row of benches, and she stumbled over people as she came out.

"I have a problem," she said, moving toward the pulpit. "I have no strength. I become weak in the afternoons. Please help me. Bring God to me to help me."

For a second Corey was taken aback, but only a second. He put his hand on the woman's head.

"God," he said. "Give her strength, give her strength all the time, give her *your* strength." He shook her head on the word *your* and seemed to push so hard the woman nearly fell over, would have fallen, except that Jamey had remained nearby and caught her and held her up.

"I can feel it," she said. "I can *feel* it! God is in me." Her back grew straighter and to Steven's complete amazement she seemed to fill in some way, almost to grow and become a healthy looking young woman.

God, he thought, *my God.* And it wasn't swearing; it was a kind of prayer. *I have seen it work,* he thought. *I have seen the miracle work.*

At that moment somebody at the side found and passed the collection basket and Steven remembered suddenly to start the final hymn. He moved to the tape player slowly, still in awe, and he saw that even his father looked stunned, kept looking at the woman as she went back to the pew, staring after her.

I saw it too, Steven thought. *She changed completely.*

Steven took the basket and Corey did the blessing and then waited for everybody to file out. Nobody moved until, finally, Jamey stood and went to the door of the tent and waved at them and walked ahead of them out into the parking area.

At that they moved out and got in their cars—all in silence, even the children—and drove away. Jamey stayed outside for a moment and spoke to the woman who had come up from the congregation and shook her hand and closed her car door for her and watched her drive away. Then he came back into the tent, where Davis—as soon as the last car was gone—started counting the collection.

"Right at three hundred dollars," he said, smiling at Jamey, who came to help count. "And some change."

Corey was drenched in perspiration, his back and sides wet. "Did you see her?" he asked of no one in particular. "Did you *see* her?"

"I did," Steven said. "It was incredible. She looked so sick and you touched her, and she just seemed to swell up with life."

Jamey looked up from helping Davis with the collection. "The woman? That was Helen."

"You know her?"

"Of course. I asked her to come. She's a filler— one of the best there is. Puffs up like a balloon, don't she? She happened to be in the area and I gave her a call. Don't you worry none—I'll pay her out of my percentage. She won't cost you a dime."

Corey held up his hand. "You mean she isn't real?"

"Well, of *course* she's real. You just saw her, didn't you? She's one of the reasons your collection did so good. I called her last night—wait a minute. You thought you'd cured one, didn't you?"

Corey didn't say anything, looking sheepish.

Jamey laughed and slapped his leg. "Oh, that's rich. Davis, listen up—he thought he'd cured one. Come in here on his first run and healed one, that's what he thought. Oh, man, that's good."

And for a second, a short second that Steven would remember later, remember a hundred times later, for three-quarters of a second he felt horrified, felt again like they had stolen something from the people in the congregation, stolen something precious, and from the look on his father's face Corey felt the same. His features fought with it; some last shred of ethics—of good—battled with all the other bad.

But only a moment. Only for the time of a dying thought did it hold. Then Corey smiled; the smile widened and turned into a laugh, and Steven smiled and started laughing a laugh he did not feel at first but again, only for a second, then louder and happier until he was doubled over with it.

"Praise God," Corey said, reaching into the collection basket and holding up a handful of money. "We are going to be *rich!*"

"Praise Almighty God," Jamey said, nodding and laughing, "from whom all blessings flow."

And Steven nodded and laughed and laughed until he could not remember the faces of the people who had sat looking up in such awe, wanting to believe, wanting to know God—laughed it all away.

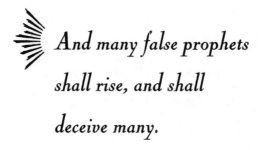

*And many false prophets
shall rise, and shall
deceive many.*

THEY EVOLVED a system, a set
of plans to follow based on Jamey's experience.

The success of the first "healing night of financial
miracles," as Corey came to call it, made them
revamp their procedure. They had been planning on
staying for a few days or even a week in each town,
but Jamey shook his head.

"They come back and see me and Davis or
Helen and it's over. You can't use the same crips
and lungers over and over, and frankly there aren't
that many good ones around. You think me and
Davis grow on trees? I learned how to twist that leg
back when I was working car accidents, and I took a
power of bumps and bruises before it started to

work right. And Davis was years and a lot of whiskey and cigarettes getting that cough right. There's many of 'em don't want to make the commitment for excellence that we do."

"I see." Corey nodded. "So we move around?"

Jamey squatted down in the dirt by the tent and nodded. "Yes, but not in a line. It has to be a star pattern, go up like this a hundred or more miles, then back down like this, then over this way."

He drew a star in the dirt with his finger. "Each point at least a hundred fifty miles from the last point so that there's no pattern. You don't want them to start following you around. That just flat ruins your chances of getting new converts to heal."

"New converts?" Steven had been standing off to the side and he moved a step closer. "You mean people to *really* heal?"

Jamey nodded. "They'll come. As the word spreads that your father has the touch, they'll come. You'll be up to your knickers in crutches and neck braces and slings."

"But Dad doesn't really heal people. It's all a sham."

Jamey looked at Corey and Davis, then back to Steven. "It's all in the head, ain't it? If they *think* they're being healed, then they're being healed, right?"

"Well . . ."

Corey cut in. "It's all psychological, Steven. I've read about it. It works."

"Just so, just so." Jamey nodded. "And once the word is out you'll see—they'll come from far and wide to get your daddy's touch. You'll have to have a truck to haul the offerings."

And he was right.

By the fourth night after the first healing sermon, Steven was so perpetually tired and confused he wasn't sure where they were or where they were going next. They traveled like a circus. As soon as the sermon was over and the collection counted, they packed the tent into the truck and started driving to the next town. When the tent was set up—

and they could do it in thirty minutes before long—
Jamey and Davis and Steven went around town with
the handbills, and Corey prepared for the night's
work by pressing his suit in the back of the tent with
an iron and small board they'd bought at a discount
store.

It all seemed a whirl to Steven. The faces came,
more and more each time as the word spread, all
looking up, all wanting to believe, all clean and
many old, most old, and after the fourth or sixth or
tenth night they didn't look different any longer. It
was the same set of faces, the same set of souls that
seemed to follow them from town to town, and at
first it bothered Steven, watching Jamey and Davis
and now and then Helen fake being healed, but then
the money was there.

Three hundred a night was the least. They went
to four, five, six, and seven hundred. Then over a
thousand a night. Two, three hundred people
jammed in the tent on more benches, standing at

the sides, begging to see, to hear, and many to be healed, and each of them brought money. More and more money.

Steven started to see fifty-dollar bills, and hundreds, and some older people who endorsed their social security checks, and he would have stopped or tried to stop Corey, but there was the money.

Corey gave him half.

"Here, you earned it." First the fifteen percent out for Jamey and Davis—they paid Helen out of their own pockets when she worked—then a small amount for motels and gas for the truck, and then Corey split it right down the middle.

Steven was making two, three, four hundred dollars a night for himself. He had money stuck in his suitcase, in his pockets, hidden all over the truck in plastic bags, and the money kept on coming. He bought new clothes, a suit so he would look good for the services, new tennis shoes, more new clothes, all the food he'd ever wanted and never

had, a new bicycle—eighteen-speed touring bike
with Campy bearings—and *still* the money came
rolling in.

"And none of it," Jamey said one evening,
watching Steven count his share, "is taxable because
it's all religious, and church money isn't taxable in
the great and wonderful country of the *Uuuu*-nited
States of A*mmm*erica. Ain't it grand?"

And there it was, thought Steven. It *was* grand
to have money. They'd been dirt poor—he almost
thought of it as *church* poor except that he realized
that none of the churches were poor—Corey just
scraping by on bad jobs and worse pay. And now
this—to have, to have money and be able to buy
things.

Was it bad, he thought, to tell people about
God and get money for it? Where did it say that you
couldn't be rich?

And his objections went. With his pockets full
of money and his stomach full of steak and malts,
and his portable video game flashing and his new

shoes and new bicycle and new life—in all that, his objections left him.

And he changed.

What was sad became funny. People in poor clothes giving their last dollar to the collection plate became hilarious; people believing in Jamey and Davis until they cried and stood with their hands in the air, waving, feeling the power of God, became something to absolutely roar about.

And as much as Steven changed, Corey changed more. In himself Steven saw the change and at first didn't like it and then accepted it and, finally, came to like what he was—rich, dressed right, smart (he thought), and very, very cool.

In his father he hated the change.

Corey became a peacock. In stages, in gradual steps and then not so gradual, he went from the man Steven had known and loved in the trailer house, sitting at the cheap table trying to figure out where to get money, to being a full-fledged strutting peacock.

He had his hair done by a professional twice a week to make it "look bigger" and sanded his shoes to show holes. He also had a suit made that looked old but wasn't, and from that point on any semblance to being poor vanished. Corey bought new expensive underwear, silk shirts, suits that set his dyed blond big hair off. He wore a gold chain under the silk shirts, socks for twenty dollars a pair, neckties for a hundred, and a set of cuff links in the shape of the cross for three hundred.

"I have to look good to bring the flock in," he explained. "If they think I'm ugly they won't come."

And the truck wasn't good enough any longer. Corey had always dreamed of getting rich, of owning a powder blue Cadillac. By the end of three weeks they had a newer, larger tent, a one-ton used but good diesel truck, and benches to hold four hundred people.

"Jamey and Davis can drive the truck," Corey said one day. "We're getting a car."

And he did. He took Steven to a dealer and

bought a used Cadillac. It wasn't powder blue—a slate gray—but it was a Cadillac, and driving it back to the tent Corey leaned back and steered with one finger and smiled. "The *oooooonnn*ly way to fly. Pure luxury."

To Steven it was like driving an aircraft carrier through traffic. But it *was* luxurious, and even when Jamey had a fit Steven thought it was a good deal.

"They see you driving that Caddy," Jamey told them, "and they'll pinch up on the collection like their hands were cut off. Nobody likes a rich minister. It's almost as bad as being fat."

"So I'll hide it. Park a block away. Who will know?"

And it worked just as Corey said. They hid the car until after the services, then Corey went for it, and he and Steven drove to the next town in soft comfort while Jamey and Davis took care of the tent and brought the truck.

It would have been enough then. There came a day when they had everything they'd ever wanted and the summer wasn't much more than half over, and the money came in buckets and there wasn't anything left to buy except more of the same, and it would have been enough.

Then Corey discovered that some of the women who came in hope of finding a reason for their faith and to see the miracle of God working through Corey were more enthusiastic than others and wanted more of Corey than just his preaching. There were not so very many of these women but some, usually one for each town, and so Corey would take an extra room at the motel and some-times stay the night, while Jamey and Davis went ahead to set up the tent. Steven would have to sleep alone or with Jamey and Davis, which he didn't like because they spent all their time watching movies where there was always a happy ending that made Jamey cry, and it would have been enough then.

Fourteen years old and sitting in your own motel room watching television, eating all the food and drinking all the pop you ever wanted, looking at your new touring bike leaning against the wall of the room, making over two hundred dollars a day to stuff in socks—all of that would have been enough for any person.

But there was a small edge still, something that would not go away, a thing that bothered him, and a day came when Steven stopped his father after the sermon was over and before he went to the motel room and left Steven alone, and he said, "When are we going to stop?"

And his father smiled and looked through the tent opening at the reason he was going to make Steven sleep alone, who was standing by her car, and he shook his head and said, "Never."

And Steven nodded and smiled and thought he meant the smile and said, "Great," and walked away and it all would have been enough.

But another thing was to happen to change it all and change his life and change Corey's life.

And the cares of this world, and the deceitfulness of riches, and the lust of other things entering in choke the Word.

"GOD *LIVES!*"

Now, Steven thought, *now it will come. He'll make the money come now. He'll start the healing.*

And Corey did as Steven thought, healing first Jamey and then Davis and then a crowd that came up on crutches and in wheelchairs.

When the healing was over, Steven turned on "Amazing Grace" for the collection and his father nodded. They had developed a new addition to the service where Steven was more a part of the collection process.

Steven stole a quick look around the tent before he went into his act. Not a bad crowd. Two hundred, maybe a little more. He had trouble judging numbers over a hundred. Once they'd had over four hundred SOBs (or souls on board, as his father put it), and Steven had thought there were more like three hundred. That had been their biggest night so far. Four hundred people in the holy tent.

He snapped his mind back. Timing was critical—timing was everything. Too soon and they just stared at him, like he was a freak or something—a fourteen-year-old freak. Too late and the moment was gone and they stared at him again—this time wondering why it took so long. Besides, if he timed it right, it started what his father called the feeding frenzy, and there were sometimes side benefits. In one small town he could never remember, a woman started to take her clothes off screaming all the while for God to come get her. It was pretty interesting until somebody—Steven thought it might have been her husband—threw a coat over her and got her out of the tent.

Now. No, wait, a few seconds. Just a few seconds more.

"He lives in me, He lives in you! God lives!" Corey cried over the sound of the stereo while Steven passed the baskets. A long breath, held for a beat, letting them think and be grateful that God lived in them and then the hook, the setting of the hook. "And *how* does He live? He lives because of your precious pledges for the Heart of the Lamb Foundation."

That was Steven's cue. He was back in the front row on the right and he stood now, both hands in the air, palms facing forward.

"YES!" he screamed. "Yes, He lives—the precious heart of the lamb lives in me!"

It was, he felt, exactly right. Sometimes he was still just that little bit off, but this time he caught it out of the corner of his eye. They shot up like robots, their hands up and facing forward while the two men with the precious Heart of the Lamb offering baskets started in the back and moved forward, sliding the baskets along and across the rows, getting the offerings—or, as his father said, milking the precious lamb.

Steven waved his arms back and forth from side to side slowly, and they all mimicked him, picking up the easy rhythm he chose, only putting their arms down to put money in a basket as it passed.

A lot of paper, he saw as it went by—some change but a lot of paper money. That was good. One night in a suburb of Dallas, they had taken in over a thousand dollars. ("A lot of *rich* sinners," his father had said. "My *favorite* kind.")

It was going well tonight. Not a thousand but several hundred, by the looks of the one basket. Enough to keep them in good food and good hotels.

God, Steven thought, *I love this. I just love this.* And he realized he'd said it out loud, jerked his head to the side and saw that the person next to him—a short man in a western shirt—was smiling and nodded and leaned over and said, "Love is what it's all about, brother."

And Steven had meant it bad, meant it the negative way, that he loved the money and the power that came from waving his hands, but the man had heard only love.

Only that.

The man actually loved, loved God and the other people in this room, and there came the edge again, the snarling corner of guilt that had been there before, and Steven nodded back at the man and looked up at the exact moment when a woman who had been healed fell. She was an elderly woman who had been in a wheelchair, crippled by arthritis, and she had stood with the help of Jamey and Davis and had even walked, and they had praised the miracle. But she fell now, along the side of the tent, and men helped her back to her chair, and Steven turned his eyes from her, almost in slow motion, turned his eyes to his father and caught it.

The same look. The edge, the hard cut of guilt,

of doubt, and when Corey saw Steven looking at him, he looked away quickly, but it was too late. Steven saw it, the look.

That night his father stayed with Steven in his room and did not leave him alone. He sat at the table reading while Steven drank Cokes and ate hamburgers and watched movies. Once Steven went up to him, during a commercial, and asked what Corey was reading, and Corey held it up to show Steven the Gideon Bible that had been in the drawer of the bedside table.

"For tomorrow's sermon," Corey said. "I'm studying for tomorrow," and he seemed about to say something more but stopped and went back to his reading.

Steven nodded but knew he was lying. He hadn't read the Bible once since he'd started preaching but made it all up as he went, letting his personality, his charisma, carry the congregation.

For two more nights he preached and healed but came back to stay with Steven and read from the

Bible, and both nights when it was time for the collection Corey turned his back when the money
came, turned his back and let Steven count it with
Jamey and Davis.

The fourth night before the sermon, Corey
came out to the three of them while they were
standing by the truck getting ready for the service,
and he stopped and looked at them and said, "I have
been reading."

"That's good," Jamey said. "Reading improves
the mind. I'll read now and then myself, you know,
when I'm of a thought to. What have you been
reading?"

"About Jesus," Corey said. "I've been reading
about Jesus Christ and what He said." He turned to
Steven. "We have to . . . we can't . . ." He trailed
off without finishing and turned away to go back
into the empty tent. Steven followed.

"What were you going to say?" Steven asked.

Corey stood by the pulpit with the crude wooden
cross and shook his head. "Nothing."

"Were you going to say this is wrong and we can't do this anymore?" Steven asked.

Corey had been looking at the side of the darkened tent and he turned suddenly to Steven. "You too?"

"It . . . bothers me. The money and the healing and the . . . women. All of it bothers me in some way I don't understand."

Corey turned toward the pulpit and didn't say anything but put his hand on the cross, looked where his fingers touched, and stood that way for a long time, in silence, looking at the cross and touching it.

"We have to stop," Steven said. "This is wrong."

"They're coming now. Start the music," Corey said, then turned and walked away, out into the parking area, where the cars were starting to pull in, and when he turned Steven saw that he was still carrying the Gideon Bible from the room in his left hand.

The service started normally, with the music

and singing, and when it was done Corey stepped up to the pulpit and held up the Bible and stood in his expensive poor suit with his expensive hair and rich underwear and opened his mouth and said, "You know what Jesus said? He said it was easier for a camel to pass through the eye of a needle than it is for a rich man to enter the kingdom of heaven." He took a breath and then removed his coat and threw it on the ground. "I have become rich by stealing," he said. "I, we, have been stealing from you, taking money in collections, healing when we knew nothing of what we were doing—we have been stealing your money but worse, much worse, we have stolen something more precious than money."

The congregation sat, stunned, some with their mouths literally open, some trying to smile as if it were a joke. Corey looked at Steven and Steven thought, *That's it, go for it,* and Steven nodded and smiled.

"We have," Corey continued, "been stealing

your faith. I do not deserve to stand up here, I do not deserve to take collections, I do not deserve anything and would not be surprised if you all got up and walked out right now."

He paused and waited but nobody got up, and he smiled.

"For those who stay, I want to talk about Jesus. Really just talk about Him. You know what He said—along with those other things I just read? I have been sitting for two nights reading what He said in this Bible, and He said, 'What shall it profit a man if he shall gain the whole world and lose his soul?'" Corey turned to Steven, looked at him, and smiled and half whispered, "He really said that. He really did."

And Steven nodded and Corey turned back to the congregation and took a breath and said, "Let's talk about that, shall we?"

And they did. They talked for two hours and then sang and the people left, leaving money on the benches even when Corey said he wouldn't take it, and when they were gone Jamey and Davis came back in and counted it.

"Seven hundred. One of the best nights and you didn't even heal nobody."

But Corey stopped him, took the money. "All of this goes into a local charity."

Jamey stared at him. "You were serious up there?"

Corey nodded. "Every word."

"You found God."

"I hope it was more that He found me."

"Can't we keep just a little?"

Corey shook his head. "Not a dime."

"Are you serious?" Jamey stared. "You mean you're going back to that trailer house and work flipping hamburgers somewhere?"

Corey nodded. "Later. First we are going to spend the rest of the summer making up for the first part of the summer." He looked at Steven. "If you don't mind, I'd like to travel around with the tent a little longer like we first started to do and just set it up and talk about God and maybe read some more about Jesus. Not for money, you understand—just to . . . well, to try and make it up, like I said."

Steven nodded.

"We'll sell the Caddy."

"And my bike."

"If you want."

"You people are nuts," Jamey said. "You're just plain nuts."

Corey nodded. "Probably. The thing is, we could still use some help—you know, setting up, putting out the word."

"For no money?"

"None. Not a penny."

Jamey frowned. "Not a chance."

"Well then . . ." Corey let it hang.

"Yeah. We'll be moving on. There's a guy over by New Orleans preaching the Word by making animals talk. They say he can make a frog spout the gospel. We'll go help him." Jamey nodded to Davis, and they walked off.

Clean and gone, Steven thought, watching them go like they came. *Just here and gone.* He turned to Corey. "Now what?"

Corey shrugged. "Like I said—let's go talk about God."

"Sounds good to me," Steven said and realized as the words came out that he really meant them. It did sound good. . . .